Rhythm and Rhyme

Moon and cookie collection

Jenith Yvonne Lashley

My little Quacker

My Quacker is quite a Quacker
And there's no better Quacker
Than my little Quacker
Who loves to swim in the middle
Of every little puddle
The rain leaves behind
I love my little Quacker
Who never seems to mind
When it's time to eat
And keeps on paddling
With his little feet
Even though he hears me calling
My little Quacker is really a good Quacker

My Little Song

Come along and help me sing my little song
You can dance, you can shout
Hop and jump around
This song is a happy song
I'm happy, happy, happy, so happy

I can sing my little song
Gee, wee ha, ha, hee, hee
I love to see the bees
As they fly all the way to their hive
'Come along'
Help me sing my little song
I'm happy, happy, happy, so happy

I love to see the horses
As they trot along
Click, clock, clickety, dee
They make me so happy you see
Come along
Help me sing my little song
I'm happy, happy, happy, so happy
As I can ever be
Happy, happy, happy...wee

The Whys

Who has the answers to all the whys?
What if there were no answers
For you and I
There would be no use to wonder... why?

What if there was no one to answer
All the questions to all the whys
What would we do?
God has all the answers
To all the whys
I'm sure he gave them
To some one too
So we don't have to wonder...
Why?

Trees

Trees tall or short
Trees in the forest
Or along our streets
Trees to shade us from the sun
Trees we can climb
And have lots of fun
… There is one in my backyard
Trees to give us paper and lumber
Furniture and houses
To even hide a hive of bees
And a place for the mother bird
To make a home for her little birdies

The Moon

Moony, moony shines so bright
It shines in the darkest night
Way up high in the sky
As it glides and slides
It bids us goodbye
Until morning light

The Stars

Why do the stars shine at night?
Why do they twinkle in the sky?
Because… they are diamonds way up high
Why do they shine so bright?
Why do the stars give us light?
Because… they are rulers of the night

The Hat Pin

My mother has a beautiful hat pin
She uses it to pin her hat upon her head
So when the wind blows
It will stay on instead
It will not fly in the wind
As though it had a pair of wings

My mother has a beautiful hat pin
She hides it in the middle of the bow
It looks like a butterfly
So I guess no one will ever know
It's a pin... not a butterfly
Hidden in the middle of her bow

The Sun

Every morning I wake up
Expecting to see the sun
As he peeps down from the sky to land
To light our way
To carry out our plan
Every morning I wake up
Expecting to see the sun
For I know I'll be able to play
And have lots of fun
We can go to the beach or the park
Or take my doggie for a walk
We can do all the things
We want to do before it gets dark

The Rainbow

Way up in the sky there's a rainbow
And outside is getting filled with dark clouds
Yet the rainbow sits pretty in the sky
Maybe it will only stay for awhile?
To let us know that rain just came by

Way up in the sky there's a rainbow
Now I know why I saw it sitting in the sky
For just as I came out to play
The rain came down and spoiled my day
But I know that the sun will shine another day

The Birds

I sat in a chair one sunny morning
Beholding the cloudless sky
I looked out my window
And saw birds as they flew by
Without a worry …Without a care
The blackbird
The sparrow
The robin
And the list goes on
From sun up to sun down
It's easy as hello and goodbye
We will be back in a little while

Two Friends

We disagree
So that we can agree
Just the two of us
We don't need another fellow
To help us
To disagree to agree

My Rain Gear

Splish, splash, splish
I love to walk in the puddles
With my blue rain shoes
When it's raining
I put on my rain coat
So I won't get soaked
I take my umbrella to cover my head
My rain gear keeps me protected
So I can stay dry
Even though it's raining outside

The Bun

I'm hot as the July sun
I'm a hot shot
I'm having fun
This is my stop
This is my spot
I can hop
I can run
I'm nothing but a hot cross bun

My Little Secret

My little secret
I hope will always be kept
And no one would ever tell
I threw my only penny down the well
I thought I would make a wish
To get plenty more pennies
And buy my mother a new dish
Which was broken in two
By my little pet bunny
I hope my little secret
Will always be kept
Between us two

My Little Doll Molly

My little doll Molly
Talks to me whenever I
Put her in her little pulley
We all go for walks
Along with my pet Polly
And mother and me in the park
The dogs would run and bark
Or roll on the green grass
Whenever we pass
While mother would stop
To say hello and have a little talk
My little doll Molly
Keeps me company
While I sit upon a little rock
My mother would chat and talk
With her sister and my Aunt Fanny
Who we met in the park as we stopped

My Little Red Hen

My little red hen
Flew over the fence
And met a dog named Ben
They both ran away together
To a place call blue den
Where once lived an old lion
Who gave up his home
To two strange friends
Off he went to find himself
A new pavilion
And never came back
To see the two strange friends
My little red hen
And the dog called Ben

An Old Horse Shoe

I once found me an old horse shoe
And hope it would bring me
Plenty of good luck
I had stumped my little toe
Looked down and picked it up
I bent over to take a look
'cause I once read in my little book
How an old man
Came into some good luck
All because he had on him
An old horse shoe
Hidden in an old rusty tin
He kept it in his pocket
Whenever he went out to fish
He pretended it was a priceless little locket
And used it when he needed to make a wish
And would always come home with the biggest fish!

The Leopard

The leopard has sprung
He is just a fierce fat cat
And he's no pet
When he's as hungry
As he can get
When he is out hunting for his prey
Who dares to stand in his way?
The leopard is just a fierce fat cat
Who can easily trample the biggest rat

The Man in the Moon

Last night I thought I saw a man in the moon
I saw him smile down at me
With big eyes and a mouth full of teeth
A nose to smell the lilies and roses
In the garden next door to me
I called him but he did not answer
 I tried to tell him
He looks just like the cookie
My mother gave to me
And my little brother Tim
I tried to wave to him
But he just looked at me and grinned
As he glided over the green pasture
Towards the hills
Away from our window sill
Out of sight where I couldn't reach him

My Idea

My idea was...
I thought the sky was blue
And not to mention
The sea couldn't help being so too
What if the sky was pink or grey?
Wouldn't the sea be that way?
Oh, no!
I can't imagine
A world without blue
Who wants to see only pink or grey?

The Four Winds

"Hey!" says the North Wind to the South Wind
I'm about to come your way
"No!" said the South Wind to the North Wind
For I too am on my way
"Hi!" said the South wind to the East wind
I bet you are going West
"Yes!", said the East Wind to the South Wind
Come along and be my guest

A Building

I went up a hill
And there I saw a building
That was being built
And oh, what a building it was
Maybe a castle or a mansion
Who cares, all I know
I went up a hill
And there I saw a building
That was being built

A little cookie

I am a little cookie
That
    likes
        to
          dance
            and
              play
And when the sun is shining
It makes my day a happy day!

The Peeping Sun

The sun rises to peep over the mountain
To see what he can see
And there's nothing hidden from his eyes
As he slowly makes his way high up into the skies
All day long he glides and slides
Until it's time to say goodbye
He leaves us with a smile
And creeps into his domain
Until it's time to rise again

Raindrops

Pitter, Patter,
Raindrops are falling on my head
Soon I'll be dripping wet
Because I forgot my umbrella on my bed
Pitter, Patter,
Raindrops are falling on my head
Each raindrop will form a puddle
Some will make a little pond
Ducks will come out to swim in the middle of the puddle
that became
a pond

Two Peas

Two peas in a pod
          Sitting green and pretty
Bursting with cheer
          Round and happy
Without a care
          Leave them alone
Until they are ripe and ready
          To burst out of their pod
Onto our plates
          And into our tummies
Yummy, yummy!

To order additional copies of
this book, contact:
Xlibris
844-714-8691
www.Xlibris.com
Orders@Xlibris.com

ISBN: Softcover   978-1-6641-9502-8
        Hardcover   978-1-6641-9503-5
        EBook   978-1-6641-9501-1

Print information available on the last page

Rev. date: 05/26/2022